CONVERGENCE
OF ODYSSEYS

CONNOR WHITELEY

No part of this book may be reproduced in any form or by any electronic or mechanical means. Including information storage, and retrieval systems, without written permission from the author except for the use of brief quotations in a book review.

This book is NOT legal, professional, medical, financial or any type of official advice.

Any questions about the book, rights licensing, or to contact the author, please email connorwhiteley@connorwhiteley.net

Copyright © 2024 CONNOR WHITELEY

All rights reserved.

DEDICATION

Thank you to all my readers without you I couldn't do what I love.

CHAPTER 1

When the *Lady Of Light* dropped out of Ultraspace, it entered a battle.

The long blade-like warship jerked, vibrated and moaned softly as I, Ithane Veilwalker, stood on the massive oval bridge watching the situation unfold. Loud flashing warning lights and alarms sounded overhead to warn the rest of our fleet what was happening, and everyone was preparing for battle stations.

We were about to go to war.

I leant on the lovely warm back of my purple crystal command throne as I focused on what was happening in the void outside. Thousands upon thousands of immense white pods that looked like white peas from this distance darted, swirled and zoomed through the void like their lives depended on it. Then even more white warships appeared to be approaching us.

I didn't know what the Imperium wanted but the

very fact that my fellow humans were here wasn't a good sign. Especially as black smoky, shadowy blade-like warships were also swarming the Imperial warships.

The entire void was a firework display of explosions, laser fire and death. Imperial warships shattered like glass and the black smoky warships of the Dark Keres exploded too and screamed out bloody murder as the Death God roared out in pleasure of consuming the souls of his followers and those of his enemies.

I flat out hated that the Dark Keres were too. Unlike my fleet that was a beautiful mixture of Keres and humans with me being a human that was brought back to life by the Goddess of Life Genetrix to serve her. The Dark Keres had sold their souls to the Death God Geneitor, a foul divine being that only wanted to consume all life in the universe and probably any universes beyond this one if such things existed.

"Battle Stations," a human male said to my left as everyone just got on with their duty.

The *Lady Of Light* continued to hum, vibrate and jerk as we were fired upon. And the foul aroma of death, burnt ozone and gunpowder filled my senses as my psychic abilities tapped into what was happening here. We were all here for a single purpose.

It didn't matter if the living soul was human, Keres or Dark Keres and it definitely didn't matter what fraction they served. We were all here for the soul purpose of something we didn't even understand.

Every living creature was having their fate and their odyssey spun and twisted and ended by a thousand different factors all pulled by Geneitor or Genetrix. They were the masters of fate and sometimes I really did feel like a puppet, but those two divine beings had led all of us here.

And I just didn't understand why.

I had been on a mission to recover one of the Soulstones, crystals that contained the souls of the 5 lesser gods of Genetrix and Geneitor, and these Soulstones were the key to resurrecting both of them. Apparently a human male had it and he was meant to be heading here.

I just didn't understand why the others were here. It made no sense.

"Brace!" a woman shouted.

I looked up and saw an immense missile scream through the void towards us.

"Have a little faith Captain," I said holding out my hand and allowing bright white tendrils of magical energy to zoom out of it.

The magic atomised the missile instantly but I had to sit down after that stunt. I wasn't used to destroying something that powerful so easily.

I sat on my delightfully warm command throne and clicked my fingers so streams upon streams of data revealed themselves. I started reading it and it was as bad as I feared.

"Have you looked at the Mother World?"

I looked up and weakly smiled at the tall female Keres standing to my left. She was as beautiful, extremely thin and elf-like as the rest of her kind but I could tell she was scared. Because this battle wasn't just happening around any world in the galaxy, this was happening around the most holy world to the Keres.

Genesis, the mother world of their kind.

I forced myself to look past my holographic data readouts, past the exploding ships and fighters in the void and I weakly smiled at Genesis. An immense green world covered in the most beautiful forests I had ever seen and I had seen photos of the planet from Imperial and Keres archives and it was sensational.

It was the most beautiful planet in the galaxy.

Yet this time it was burning.

I stood up as I noticed entire continents were ablaze sending immense black columns of choking, toxic smoke high into the atmosphere. This was one of the most outrageous sights I had ever seen and this wasn't just a physical insult against the natural beauty in the galaxy. This was an attack against the mind, spirit and history of the entire Keres race.

That explained why the Imperium wanted to annihilate it.

"The Motherworld is lost," I said standing up to face the entire bridge.

CHAPTER 2

Commander Jerico Nelson flat out couldn't believe what the hell he had let himself get involved in for the sake of honouring the dying wish of a dead friend. He hadn't really minded the same dead friend "gifting" him the necklace that was meant to combine the so-called soul of a God (what rubbish) but he didn't want to get involved with a war over a planet by three different sides.

Jerico shook his head as he leant against the cold, perfectly smooth brown bark of an almost straight tree with thousands of little branches shooting off in all directions. Jerico had never seen small diamond-shaped leaves before that glittered in the orange, yellow and red light coming from the flames sweeping across the entire planet.

Jerico knelt down on the cool muddy ground on the edge of the cliff and just shook his head as he saw the raging inferno that was devouring the valley below him. It must have been a good two kilometres down to the valley floor but Jerico could only watch as trees, plants and Keres were devoured by the dancing flames.

He flat out didn't believe in all this rubbish about the Keres Gods and Goddesses but he couldn't deny something wasn't natural about those flames. They were surely too big, too controlled and it looked like they were dancing too much for them to be natural.

The sound of the roaring, crackling, popping flames was deafening and Jerico was so looking forward to getting off this planet. Jerico loved how beautiful it had been a day or two ago but it was monstrous now.

He wasn't even sure what had happened. He had arrived yesterday to try and find out more about this Ithane Veilwalker woman but no one seemed to know her and then Imperial and Dark Keres ships had appeared at the exact same moment. It wasn't right, it wasn't natural and Jerico couldn't help but feel like something much larger was going on here.

An explosion overhead made Jerico reach for his sniper rifle and machine gun as he saw fresh explosions light up the smoky black sky. He wasn't sure but Jerico could have sworn these were new explosions that were slightly different to the explosions he had been watching for hours.

Maybe there were new players or ships or even armies here. He really hoped that wasn't true, he didn't want anyone else to die and he was sure this world was going to become his tomb.

Jerico smiled as the necklace containing the so-called Keres God of Hope Spero pulsed bright white and sent warmth into him. Jerico supposed he was going to miss this necklace and its weird abilities when he met this Ithane woman but he had to honour his dead friend.

"Arms up," a woman's voice said to him.

Jerico rolled his eyes and slowly turned around to see a female Keres standing behind him. She was definitely from this planet with her smooth beautiful skin, extremely thin, unnatural humanoid features and long blond hair that crackled with golden magical energy.

"I am a friend of the Keres," Jerico said not sure if she was going to believe him.

"Impossible. No human is a friend of ours. Look at what you have done to our world," the woman said.

Jerico frowned as the air crackled with black magical energy and he really didn't want her to kill him. He had to complete his mission.

"I'm looking for Ithane Veilwalker. Do you know her? I'm meant to give something to her, can I show you?" Jerico said.

The woman hesitated but after the longest moments of his life, she nodded and Jerico revealed the still-glowing necklace to her.

She smiled and the air stopped crackling immediately, but Jerico noticed the foul taste of iron, rust and sweat had formed in his mouth.

"Ithane Veilwalker you say," the woman said like it was a joke. "My forces tell me she's just arrived in orbit with her entire fleet,"

Jerico had no idea who the hell this Ithane woman was but he wasn't sure about her. It wasn't exactly easy to get a fleet of your own these days between the human-Keres war, the evil control of Rex's Imperium and limited resources everyone had during wartime.

Jerico just hoped beyond hope this Ithane person wasn't a criminal, pirate or a servant of the Rex. If that happened then he might even have to break his oath to his dead friend, something he wanted to avoid at all costs.

An explosion overhead made Jerico jump and he looked and saw five white pods scream towards the valley next to him. The annihilated pods smashed into the sides of the valley's cliff and they exploded.

The battle was getting worse.

Jerico looked at the woman. "We have to find Ithane Veilwalker. Can you take me to her?"

"Maybe," the woman said. "My name is Piper by the way. A forced name your Rex gave me when he enslaved my homeworld during the First Human-Keres war,"

"Jerico Nelson is my name and I don't serve the Rex anymore. I stopped serving him a long time ago,"

Jerico wasn't sure if Piper believed him but as more explosions roared overhead she gestured him to follow her.

And Jerico just hoped beyond hope he wasn't trusting the wrong Keres. Sometimes it was impossible to tell Light from Dark Keres.

A possible mistake Jerico hoped wouldn't cost him his life.

CHAPTER 3

In both my lives, including my human life before I became Genetrix's will incarnate, I have never ever heard anything as scary as an entire bridge full of humans and Keres go deadly silent leaving only the roaring, humming and vibrating bangs of a ship in the background as it's under attack.

I don't know even think I had meant to say it out loud but I had, and now the awful foul aromas of death, burnt ozone and gunpowder filled my senses even more and left the disgusting taste of raw meat form on my tongue.

The situation was definitely getting worse by the minute.

I frowned as I saw everyone step away from their terminals, scanners and battle stations and they focused on me. The humans looked scared and concerned but the Keres looked outraged and like I was almost as bad as the Dark Keres themselves.

"The Motherworld cannot be lost," a male Keres

said. "That world is a shrine to our past and it is a reminder that the Keres once ruled the stars. We once had the mightiest empire in Galactic history,"

"Exactly," someone else said.

"And that is why we have to save it," a human woman said.

The entire ship roared as our gun turrets unleashed a volley of shots. We were running out of time and the enemy was well aware of our presence by now.

"Negative," I said. "Genetrix brought me back to life because everything I do is about preserving and protecting life. That is what we have to do now,"

Everyone nodded.

"The Goddess of Life brought us here to find the human with the Soulstone belonging to Spero, God of Hope. We find him, get the Soulstone and get out," I said channelling as much as Genetrix's influence as I could.

A Keres female shook her head. "What about the people on the planet? Don't their lives matter?"

I nodded for a brief moment because this was the problem about being in charge of the Daughters of Genetrix. I was our leader and our Goddess' Will incarnate. I had to make the impossible decisions.

"Better to let them sacrifice themselves for the Goddess then annihilate our entire fraction trying to save them. Because if we die then who will stop the Dark Keres from resurrecting Geneitor and him devouring all life?"

The Keres female backed down and I hated myself as I tapped into the psychic echo of the battle around me. And I heard those Keres scream out in agony as some of their souls were thankfully saved but others had their own devoured and tortured by Geneitor.

I didn't want to stay here any longer than needed.

I clicked my fingers and the air crackled with magical energy as a map of the situation appeared and I gestured over two of my most senior Captains, one Keres, one human woman. Everyone else went back to their battle stations.

I hissed as the smell of death, burnt ozone and gunpowder grew even more.

"My Lady," one of the captains said, "Imperial and Dark Keres forces have touched down on Genesis. They seem to be torturing, taking prisoners and obliterating our monuments,"

"Where is the human?" I asked surprised that I sounded almost fully Keres then instead of a strange mixture of the two.

"Unknown," the woman said. "Can't you just tap into the psychic stuff and just pinpoint him?"

I laughed and gestured towards the battle outside. "There are thousands of people dying and their souls screaming out in the void every minute of this battle. This battle alone stretches across an entire planet and the space surrounding it. Do you really think I can just pluck a non-magical mind out of all that psychic noise easily?"

"Maybe?" she asked.

I saluted her because I really did like her attitude. It was good she wasn't scared to ask questions.

The damn ship roared as a volley of missiles slammed into us. I grabbed one of the captains as the ship jerked so hard she fell over.

"Status!" I shouted.

"Sheilds will last for another ten minutes. Everyone is starting to turn their attention on us. We're already lost 10% of the fleet," a man said but I couldn't see him.

I looked at my Captains and I knew I was going to have to do this alone and I wasn't going to have that much time to do it.

"My lady we have to make a move now," the woman said.

"Agreed," I said going over to the back of my command throne and picking up my two swords. "If our target is anywhere he would have made it to the planet and I suspect he would be in the thickest of the fighting,"

"Why?" a woman asked as another volley smashed into the ship.

I clicked my fingers and an immense golden portal appeared in front of me. "Because our Odysseys are converging Genetrix and Geneitor want me and this man to find each other. I don't know why but the Gods want me and him to be united,"

"And that's what scares me," a number of people said as one.

"Just buy me as much time as you can," I said as I stepped through the portal.

And I had to admit this divine game I was stepping into was terrifying me a lot more than I ever wanted to admit.

CHAPTER 4

The thick aromas of incredibly juicy steak, freshly roasted garlic and deep fried pork filled Jerico's senses as he followed Piper through an immense Keres city. This had to be one of the biggest he had ever had the pleasure of seeing. Jerico had always liked how the large purple-crystal towers that rose up like daggers from the ground were formed so seamlessly that each tower was a work of art in itself.

Jerico really doubted any human could create something so breathtaking, but as he followed Piper between two large towers, he saw that this city had already been attacked.

He saw the scorched marks on the top of the towers and the streams of blood that flooded through the city. Jerico hated seeing the Keres, they were only innocent aliens trying to live in a galaxy they had once owned. It was only because the Rex in his stupidity had been terrified by their peaceful magic that he had decided to wipe them out.

Jerico tried to smile at the small groups of tall extremely thin Keres in blue robes as he went past them. They didn't react, they didn't smile, they only watched him like he was the biggest threat to their lives.

Maybe he was. Back when he had served with the Imperial Army, Jerico had fought, killed and burnt more Keres cities than he ever cared to admit.

He just hoped he could save or do something, anything for this one.

"In here," Piper said without turning around.

Jerico followed her inside one of the purple towers and suddenly found himself on the top floor overlooking the entire city. He was surprised there was only a purple crystal floor, there were no walls or windows that his human mind could see. He supposed this was probably some kind of Keres magic because he could still feel the warm breeze against his cheeks but he had a 360-degree view of his surroundings.

Piper smiled next to him and then Jerico noticed there were six other Keres standing in the middle of the floor. He recognised five of them in their thin golden metal armour as some kind of guards, but the central figure was brand-new in her crimson red robes of office.

Jerico didn't recognise the golden chain she wore around her neck and the bronze staff barely looked strong enough to hold, let alone support any weight. Jerico doubted it had a practical use.

"Great Mother," Piper said, "tell me some good news,"

Jerico had never heard of a Great Mother before, he had no idea what she did in Keres society but she looked important and Jerico really hoped she wasn't going to be an obstacle. He had to get to Ithane.

"Excuse me," Jerico said.

"I know who you are before you say anything human," the Great Mother said. "You are Commander Jerico Nelson, murderer of Keres and a servant of the Rex,"

The five guards instantly whipped swords out of nothing and pointed them at Jerico.

"I am no such thing anymore," Jerico said knowing he couldn't survive a fight. "I am sorry for what I did for the Rex before I knew any better but I want to help you. I really do,"

Jerico gestured them towards the necklace and the Great Mother grinned and clapped her hands.

The guards put away their swords and Jerico cocked his head as he blinked and found the guards were sitting in front of five very human-looking computers.

Piper went straight over to them like the guards were working on an impossible computer problem.

"What's wrong?" Jerico asked joining them.

"The clocks have stopped. The magic has stopped. Everything has stopped," the Great Mother said. "As soon as the Dark Keres and Imperial forces arrived all the clocks on Genesis stopped working and even our magic is spotty,"

Jerico had no idea what the hell was happening. He knew the Keres weren't stupid for their technology to not work, and as far as he knew all the Keres's technology was tied to the universe itself similar to the Atomic Clock back on Earth. This made no sense.

"We've tried to contact the Keres homeworlds but we can't reach them," a guard said.

"Maybe there's interference," Jerico said.

The Great Mother laughed. "No human. You don't understand. We cannot get any messages out using our technology, our magic, our faith. Something extremely powerful is making sure we don't exist in the universe. It's almost like…"

"What?" Jerico asked looking straight at her.

The Great Mother shook her head and Jerico knew this was bad. He supposed Great Mothers were some kind of ancient leadership role in the Keres and given how long the Keres lived, Jerico was sure this one was ancient.

But she looked scared. In his experience people with lots of years of experience don't get scared unless it's truly warranted.

"What?" Jerico asked coldly.

It's almost like," the Great Mother said looking around, "something is trying to take us out of Reality. Reality is where time is, magic is and everything the Keres rely on,"

Jerico shook his head. He sort of understood

what that meant. He had seen a lot of impressive stuff over his military career and he knew the Keres were capable of doing some crazy, impossible things but taking an entire planet out of existence that seemed impossible even for the Keres.

Maybe not a God.

Jerico shook the stupid idea away because there were no such things as Gods or Goddesses. It was simply Keres' stories to give them hope in the face of extinction.

"This human needs to find something called Ithane Veilwalker," Piper said.

"I felt the presence of her fleet arrive," the Great Mother said, "but she isn't there anymore. Not in orbit and there is too much psychic interference but she searches for you too,"

Jerico had no idea why a possibly dangerous woman with her own fleet would be hunting him. He knew nothing of this woman and yet he was meant to handover a so-called powerful necklace. As much as Jerico wanted to honour his dead friend, he had to admit this was seeming more and more dangerous.

"Imperial Forces!" a guard shouted looking at his computer screen.

"Bastards," Jerico said taking out his machine gun.

"We don't have the soldiers to protect everyone," the Great Mother said. "Sound the alarm. Get everyone into the tunnels,"

"It will take too long to save everyone," Piper

said.

Jerico pointed his machine gun away from the guards. "Where are they? How much time do you need?"

The Great Mother grinned. "As much time as you and Genetrix can give me,"

"Then you will have it," Jerico said storming off towards the coordinates Piper had given him.

Jerico just hoped he could save some innocent lives.

CHAPTER 5

Something was extremely wrong as I stepped out of my golden portal and the deafening screams of men, women and Keres alike filled my ears like a choir of the dead was right next to me. I tried to cover my ears but the screams of the death only got louder and louder as my magic struggled to adjust to the sheer amount of death happening on Genesis.

I collapsed to my knees and barely felt the cold rough roots in the ground as images of the faces of the dead flashed across my mind. I knew Genetrix was trying to sweep up their souls as best she could before Geneitor grabbed them and devoured and them forever.

I couldn't believe sometimes what Genetrix had to go through daily just to protect and preserve life as much as possible. I know she's a Goddess but I would never tell another soul this but I do feel her pain at times. Sometimes when I try to use magic I get hit by crippling pain and sadness and I realise

Genetrix's suffering.

And that puts the fear in the Goddess into me. If a Goddess like Genetrix can despair at the state of the galaxy then I seriously question what the hell I can do about it.

Silence.

I forced myself to take a wonderfully sweet, fruity breath of the cool Genesis air as I stood up and placed my hands firmly on the hilts of my swords. I had to be alert here and I couldn't afford to make a single mistake.

Genesis had to be one of the most beautiful, stunning worlds I've ever had the privilege of seeing. I had to be standing on some kind of beautiful clifftop with a valley thousands of metres below me.

The valley itself was stunning with large straight trees with little boat-shaped copper leaves that shone in the dying light of Genesis. They gently hit each other as a warm gust of wind travelled past me and down into the valley, it made the light sparkle and even sang a little like windchimes.

It was so beautiful.

I didn't know how far away I was from the nearest battle but I could feel the psychic pressures of thousands of unclaimed souls starting to press against my mind again. I wanted so badly to help Genetrix collect them to spare the souls from being devoured, but I had to get out of here.

I couldn't risk the lives of my forces any longer than absolutely necessary.

I started into the forest away from the clifftop. I couldn't help but smile as these trees were even more beautiful than the others below me. Their tall trunks were crimson red like metal with blood red diamond-shaped leaves that sparkled in the sunlight.

And the smell was great. The senses of maple syrup, strawberries and chocolate overwhelmed my nose. It was some of the best smells I had ever walked through before.

"My Lady," my Ship mistress said into my mind. "We have a problem onboard,"

I have to admit that April might have lived, slept and worked down in the very heart of the *Lady of Light* and she might have been a figure of myth amongst the crew because she made a point of never seeing them. But she always knew when to bother me.

"What?" I asked.

"There is something closing in on us in Ultraspace. Something like a massive shadow that is swimming towards us," April said.

I rolled my eyes. This seriously wasn't what we needed because if something was in Ultraspace, the intergalactic network humans used to travel faster than light, then I really didn't want to know how this would affect our escape.

But I knew I was going to have to find out.

"What are you saying?" I asked.

"Someone or something is trying to cut off our escape into Ultraspace. I doubt the Imperial forces will notice it but I am watching it. We might have to go into the Nexus,"

"Make the preparations," I said a lot harsher than I meant to. "Be careful and the Goddess Protects,"

"May she guide our hand like she guides mine," April said cutting off the mental link.

I shook my head at the very idea of having to go into the Nexus, the Keres version of Ultraspace which was actually a lot faster, safer and less infected with Geneitor's taint, considering the reports I've had lately.

It turned out some Dark Keres had managed to tap into the Nexus recently so it wasn't as much as of a safe haven for the Keres anymore. Instead thousands of Dark Keres followers had taken to storming, pirating and obliterating all vessels they came across.

I had a feeling we were going to have enough casualties in this battle over Genesis. I didn't want to get involved in any more battles than I had to. And the Nexus was hopefully one I could avoid.

I had to focus on my mission.

"Guide me to my target Mother of Life," I said as I closed my eyes and allowed my magic to tap into the psychic nightmare that had been generated by the battle.

All I had to do was pick out a single human mind out of this entire nightmare of war.

I hissed as I tapped into the screams, explosions and cries for help that filled Genesis and its orbit. So many thousands of people were dying and killing in each passing minute and each action created an echo in the psychic field I was tapping into.

I hated how this wasn't going to work. There were simply too many minds, too many deaths, too many incidents of Geneitor trying to seek me out to so he could send his forces to kill me.

Maybe I was going to have to focus on the so-called Soulstone this mere man was meant to be carrying. I was going to be so pissed if this was a ruse but I doubted it. And the least I could do was save this man's life and protect his soul like Genetrix wanted.

I shifted my psychic focus and searched for any magical signatures or souls that were too bright to be a death or a Keres. I didn't bother looking for human souls because theirs were simply too dim in the grand scheme of things.

I saw it.

I wasn't sure how many kilometres away it was but there was a massive bright white beacon in the psychic nightmare. It could have been a massacre and a mass release of souls but I didn't want to believe it.

As much as I wanted to teleport there I knew Geneitor could see my teleportations and if the man was there, I was not going to lead the enemy to him.

I had to find, protect and save this man no matter the cost.

As I went towards my target through the crimson red forest, I couldn't help but feel like I was taking one step closer to something far darker and more terrifying than I ever thought possible.

Later on I wish I had listened to myself at this moment.

CHAPTER 6

As much as Jerico appreciated Piper's offer of a hundred Keres soldiers, he made her send them deeper into the city so they could protect the innocent Keres running for the tunnel network.

Jerico lay down on his stomach with Piper doing the same to his left as he aimed his sniper scope at the Imperial forces below them. Jerico liked being on top of a cliff with a charred blackened valley below him.

Another benefit of the position, which was all that Jerico cared about, was how there was a lot of crimson red tree cover behind them. He hoped he didn't wouldn't need it but Jerico wanted that to be a good escape route in case they got caught.

He had chosen this position to attack the hundreds of Imperial army forces in their foul sterile white armour because the valley narrowed behind them. So the Imperial forces would have to slow and that would make them easy to shoot.

Jerico didn't like the awful black smoke and hints

of charred flesh that invaded his lungs but he was a commander. He knew exactly how to snipe the enemy into submission. The key was to find the enemy's leadership and kill them before the enemy knew what was going on.

Then it was a simple task of destroying the enemy before they recovered from the crippling loss.

"I don't see a captain," Piper said.

Jerico kept searching the hundreds upon hundreds of white-armoured humans for any sign of a commander or captain. He was a sniper and snipers were always patient.

And if push came to shuff then he would simply get Piper to blow up the sides of the valley near where it narrowed.

"What's your real name?" Jerico asked.

Piper laughed. "After the First Human-Keres war and the Keres leader signed the Treaty of Defeat the Keres language was erased. You could only speak Imperial and so our names became Imperial,"

Jerico felt his throat dry and his stomach twist into a painful knot. He hated that he had been apart of that evil war.

"I'm sorry," Jerico said knowing it was meaningless.

"It's okay, really. You were just following rules and believing the Rex's lies like the rest of your race. You're here now and that's what matters,"

Jerico nodded and he kept searching. As far as he was concerned all the Imperial soldiers looked the same in their sterile white armour and none of them had any medals or symbols on them.

"I'm starting to search towards the back of the battle force," Jerico said.

"Why are you really here?" Piper asked searching the battle force with some weird Keres rifle.

"I told you. A dead friend wanted me to find Ithane Veilwalker, give her this so-called God and make sure she's okay,"

"You really don't believe do you?"

Jerico just looked at her. "You actually believe the Keres's Gods and Goddesses are real?"

"Of course. The Keres get their magic from Geneitor or Genetrix. And they guide our actions, and they protect us in their own way. I was a young adult when a human first tried to kill me because I was starving and I wanted a loaf of bread. That adult would have snapped my neck but he flexed his muscles and his own neck broke,"

"Okay?"

"That had to be the work of Genetrix. A human snapping their own neck instead of mine," Piper said like this was all true.

Jerico just wasn't sure. It sounded so made-up and fake but she was helping him so Jerico smiled and went back to finding his target.

He found her.

There was a woman towards the very back of the Imperial Forces wearing much thicker white metal armour with a bright red cross over her chest breast.

It was the symbol of the Rex, maybe one of his chosen, maybe one of his Hand.

If that was true then Jerico had no idea what was going on here. A Hand of The Rex did not leave Earth or enter a battlefield without any extremely good reasons and even their mere presence normally showed the Imperium had already won.

Jerico looked into Piper's eyes. "Do your people have any ships or shuttles to help them get off world?"

"No. The Treaty of Defeat meant this planet couldn't have any so-called advance technology,"

"Bastards," Jerico said lining up the woman in his sights. "We need to kill that woman with the cross on her chest,"

"Got her,"

"On three," Jerico said having a really bad feeling about this.

"One. Two,"

"Three,"

Jerico and Piper fired. The bullets silently zoomed towards the woman then nothing.

The woman was alive, smiling and looking directly at Jerico.

Something screamed overhead.

Jerico looked up.

An immense fireball was flying right towards them.

"Run!" Piper shouted.

Jerico ran into the crimson forest and just hoped

when that fireball hit it wouldn't kill them both.

CHAPTER 7

Something was definitely wrong with this entire planet as I went through a forest with crimson red trees. They were sort of beautiful but there wasn't a doubt in my mind that there was some kind of corruption was going on here.

It was the small things that gave it away really. As I went through the forest, I noticed how the closer I (hopefully) got to my target, the more the trees bent to one side and the roots cracked the soft ground like they were wanting to attack or something.

It certainly didn't relax me that I could have sworn the roots were turning in my direction as I passed. I didn't dare get too close to them in case they grabbed me or something, and I couldn't tell the time at all.

Normally I was a pretty good judge of time and how long I had been doing something for, even before Genetrix had rebirth me, I was pretty good at it. But all I felt was confusion, coldness and like my connection to the Goddess of Life was being dampened.

I might have had my connection cut from her before, I might have been filled with her divine power on other occasions but this time, it felt odd. My skin was chilling more with each passing minute (I guessed) and my magical senses were weakening.

I just had no idea why.

I shook the silly idea away and I just kept going towards my target in the forest. The trees were definitely bending more now and their little leaves just fell off their branches instead of creating sweet music.

Then they turned to ash.

The foul smell of death, gunpowder and sweat filled my senses as I continued. I was almost tempted to try and connect to Genetrix to ask her a question or two but I couldn't afford to brighten my soul in case Geneitor was watching for me closely. My soul would already be bright enough because of my magic, I didn't need to brighten it even more.

He and his servants would find me quickly enough. I had no doubt about that.

The air crackled with black magical energy as five black portals opened around me and I just stopped in my tracks as five Dark Keres stepped out.

I almost shivered in disgust of their twisted forms of their cousins. I had always liked how artfully, beautifully and humanoid the Keres were, but the Dark Keres around me looked awful with black veins pulsing black light across their skin.

Their faces looked beaten, sliced and scarred. They looked monstrous and even their black armour looked twisted and corrupted.

A black flaming sword appeared in their right hand.

I whipped out my two swords and with a thought I made them become engulfed in white cleansing flames.

"Why are the Dark Keres here?" I asked wanting to know why the enemy was actually here.

"It is the Will of the Death God," one of them said psychically so I couldn't tell who it was.

"Then why bring the Imperium?" I asked. "Geneitor wants a fight with the Daughter of Genetrix. It makes no sense for him to bring in another fraction, much less a human fraction,"

All the Dark Keres laughed around me and I realised I had made a mistake. In the original battle between Geneitor and Genetrix, it had been the Goddess of Life that had created the Keres as her army. Yet Geneitor had created humanity to kill in his name, so I just shook my head.

Geneitor could influence the humans a lot more than the Keres. I wasn't sure Geneitor actually believed the Keres could win against my Daughter of Genetrix, much less me.

So he twisted the fate of the Imperium to bring them to this moment, this battle, this point of convergence.

A single point in history where the three greatest

forces of the galaxy met and fought. I still didn't understand why or what Geneitor was planning.

The Dark Keres charged at me.

I leapt up.

I felt the Goddess's power fill me.

I swung my sword.

Two Dark Keres swung too.

I slashed their chests.

They exploded.

The other three leapt into the air.

Their supernatural agility guiding their actions.

They swung their swords supernaturally fast.

I ducked.

They kicked.

They punched.

They swung.

I dodged.

Again.

Again.

They swung.

Their swords a blur of motion.

I couldn't see their swords.

They kicked me.

Knocking me forward.

A Dark Keres appeared in front of me.

She swung her sword.

Torrents of flame shot out my fingers.

She screamed in agony.

I spun around.

Swinging my swords.

I beheaded the last two remaining Dark Keres.

Their corpses turned to ash and I just frowned as I felt the cold isolating presence of Geneitor as he devoured their souls. But I couldn't mess around anymore the Death God had known exactly where I was and I knew April was busy preparing for us to go into the Nexus back on the *Lady Of Light*.

I had to get to my target now and get us off this forsaken planet before all was lost.

Because something was coming. I didn't know what it was but something was coming for all of us and I had no idea what Geneitor was planning but this felt like a trap.

A massive trap and that utterly terrified me.

CHAPTER 8

The fireball smashed into the clifftop.

Jerico hissed as he ran as fast as he could into the crimson forest. He kept running. Maybe he could survive.

Moments later he felt the immense shockwave grab him and threw him forward like he was made from paper. Jerico hated the extreme heat that covered him as he zoomed past the crimson trees.

He couldn't see Piper. He tried to move but the force of the shockwave made that impossible. He was shocked he didn't hit anything.

The screaming roaring sound of wind passing him made him feel sick and like he was lost but then he noticed there was only pure white golden light ahead.

He bent his arms and tried to throw his weight forward as he guessed he was about to hit the ground or something.

He couldn't. It wasn't working.

His necklace glowed bright white and Jerico felt something wrap around him like a blanket.

He started running out of instinct and he felt the soft ground under his feet. He ran for about ten metres before rolling onto the ground.

A strange warmth gripped him and Jerico couldn't help but smile in relieve. He doubted the Gods were real but that necklace definitely was amazing and Jerico loved that so-called magic.

Jerico got up and his mouth dropped as he saw in the distance a hurricane of crimson trees swirling, twirling and whirling around where the shockwave had ripped them out of the ground.

Jerico just shook his head. This wasn't natural. This was making little sense but he knew there had to be some kind of foul magic at play here because that fireball should have killed them.

"Jerico," Piper said weakly.

Jerico looked around and rushed across the wide opening in the forest the hurricane had created. He saw her lying on the ground holding her stomach tight.

Then Jerico knelt down next to her and gasped. There was a large branch into her stomach and dark red rich blood was dripping out of the wound.

"I saved you," Piper said, her eyes not able to focus on him.

Jerico nodded his thanks but he had to save her. He didn't care he had only just met her, she was an innocent person and she had to be saved. Her life mattered to someone and that was all Jerico cared about.

He padded down his armour but he didn't have anything to heal her with. He was a fighter not a medic.

A loud whooshing filled the air and Jerico grabbed his machine gun that had landed a few metres from Piper. A large white pod-like shuttle was zooming towards them.

"I'll protect you," Jerico said as he prepared for the white pod to land.

"Go," Piper said. "Get to the Great Mother. You have to save the others. Leave me,"

Jerico shook his head as the white pod banked a little and it started to land ten metres in front of him. Jerico aimed his machine gun at the doors.

"Please Jerico. My life is not worth you dying. The Goddess has plans for you. She never would have allowed Spero to fall into your hands if you were unimportant,"

"Shut up about your Gods for one minute. I am going to save you," Jerico said.

A small white walkway came out of the white pod and Jerico opened fired but his bullets smashed into a purple shield of some kind as five men in sterile white armour came out.

Jerico recognised their weapons instantly. These were special forces and their long blades functioned as guns and swords with equal deadliness.

Jerico hated this position. It was too open, too

vulnerable and too deadly. He never would have picked this if he could help it. But he was determined to save Piper somehow.

"In the name of the holy Rex you Commander Jerico Nelson are a heretic and traitor to the Imperium," they all said as one. "We are ordered to kill you and bring back the Spero,"

Jerico couldn't believe all that anyone was interested in was this damn necklace. It couldn't even be that important.

The necklace glowed a little like it was laughing at him.

Jerico fired.

Bullets screamed through the air.

They smashed into the Imperial armour but Jerico gasped as the armour didn't even dent.

The men looked at each other and they nodded.

They smashed their swords on the ground. They cracked with blue electrical energy. They thrusted out their weapons towards Jerico.

Electrical energy shot towards him.

Again.

Again.

Jerico rolled to one side.

He rolled again.

The electrical energy kept coming out.

Jerico jumped.

He rolled.

He leapt.

The ground exploded in front of him.

Next to him.

Behind him.

Jerico just stopped.

He fired his machine gun.

Bullets screamed towards the enemy.

The bullets melted as electrical energy hit them.

The enemy fired.

Bullets smashed into Jerico.

Throwing him backwards.

His armour cracked and flew off him.

Jerico landed with a cold thud and he tried to move but his body ached and crippling pain filled his entire body.

He watched as one man stormed out to him whipping out a blood red dagger that he was fairly sure was meant to kill him.

Jerico tried to move. He tried to fire his machine gun. He tried everything to move.

He couldn't. His body protested with every movement. He was going to die.

The man knelt on Jerico's chest and Jerico screamed in agony as something broke inside him. Agony filled him and Jerico couldn't help but scream louder and louder as the man pressed the dagger against his throat.

A deafening whoosh echoed around him and out of the corner of his eye Jerico could have sworn a golden portal had opened.

And a very human-looking woman was stepping out of it.

Jerico just hoped whoever this woman was wasn't going to kill him. Something he seriously doubted.

CHAPTER 9

As soon as I stepped out of the golden portal I just knew this was the moment everything had been leading up to. My rebirth, my fight and my odyssey across the stars had led me to this damn moment.

I looked with utter rage at the stupid Imperial special force operatives in their pathetic white armour as they stood there staring at me like I was a mystery. They didn't know whether to kill me or save me or even protect me.

I was going to show them the error of their ways for sure. I was going to slaughter them in this large unnaturally empty clearing.

There was one operative pressing a blade against the throat of a man. I didn't know him but I noticed the pure divine energy radiating out of this necklace. He was my target. He was my divine mission and these foul Imperials were going to die.

A female Keres screamed out in pain.

I glared at her. I couldn't believe the enemy had

injured her and thrusted a branch through her stomach.

I had had it with these Imperial scum.

I whipped out my swords engulfing them in golden crackling flames.

I flew at the enemy.

They raised their guns.

They fired.

Bullets screamed towards me.

I melted them with a thought.

I swung my sword in the air.

Torrents of white cleansing flame launched themselves at the enemy.

Three operatives screamed in crippling pain as they melted.

I charged towards my holy mission.

The operative went to split the man's throat.

I thrusted a hand out in his direction.

The man hissed as he couldn't move his arm.

I charged at him.

I leapt into the air.

I spun myself and my swords.

Beheading the man instantly.

His corpse collapsed and my target stood up and wearily pointed his machine gun at me.

I ignored him and I looked at the last remaining Imperial operative. I burrowed into his mind. I saw his past, his family, his homeworld.

He collapsed to the ground and I could feel his fear wash over me again and again. I didn't care. I was here to save lives and if he had any information that might help me then I was going to find it.

Sadness washed over me and I hesitated giving the stupid operative the chance he needed to slip free of my control and snap his own neck.

As his corpse fell to the ground I shook my head and as much as I wanted to go over to my target who was still pointing his machine gun at me. I went over to the Keres woman.

I knelt down next to her and was a little surprised by the sheer icy coldness of the soft mud. The mud was part water, part blood and her skin was ghostly white. The evil branch was large and I was sure it had raptured a lot of organs.

I placed my hands over the branch and I closed my hands.

"Please Goddess of Life let me heal her so she may fight in your name once more," I said as I forced my magic into her body.

The woman didn't resist which was a relief. My mind filled with images of cells, her muscle fibres and her organs being destroyed by the dark magic inside the branch. I had no idea how it had gotten there but the dark magic was killing her even more than the branch itself.

I poured bright white cleansing light into her body and the woman screamed out in pain. She never begged me to stop and I wouldn't have listened anyway.

I had to save her.

The images in my mind showed the cells, muscle fibres and her organs were healing. The branch was dissolving and within a minute she was healed.

"Who are you?" the Keres woman asked.

I opened my eyes and just grinned as I saw she was perfectly healed.

"At least Geneitor will not have your soul today," I said smiling. "I am Lady Ithane Veilwalker of the Daughters of Genetrix,"

"Ithane?" the man asked behind me.

I turned around and I just smiled at the most beautiful man I had ever seen. I hadn't had a chance to look at the man before but… he was sensational.

My heart pounded in my chest. My swords were slippery in my hands because of the sweat and my mouth went dry for a few seconds before my magic forced my body to return to normal.

I couldn't help but focus on how cute, beautiful and insanely hot this man was with his large biceps, strong jawline and those deep emerald eyes. He was stunning to look at and I seriously wanted to kiss him but I had a mission to do.

And I had lives to save.

His necklace glowed bright white and I laughed as I knew Spero was saying hello to me. He recognised a servant of his Mother and I could feel so much warmth fill my body (some of it was from being in the presence of this stunner) as Genetrix was pleased to see her child again.

"Are you really Ithane Veilwalker?" the man

asked.

I nodded and I felt like my life had just changed forever.

CHAPTER 10

Jerico flat out couldn't believe this was the woman he had travelled all over the galaxy for. She had to be the most beautiful woman he had ever seen. Her eyes were so kind, life-filled and her long golden hair was just divine and he so badly wanted to run his hands through it.

He had been expecting Ithane to be a Keres woman or some kind of evil, monstrous servant of the so-called Death God. But he was amazed at how kind she was, she had focused on healing Piper above all else and he just had to respect her for that.

And Ithane was a stunner in that golden armour of hers. Jerico liked how it highlighted her fit, sexy body and Jerico really wanted to know how hard her body was and what it would feel against his own. He couldn't help but grin like a schoolboy. Jerico really liked this woman.

"I am Ithane Veilwalker," the hot woman said, "and I think fate brought our Odysseys together,"

Jerico rolled his eyes and Ithane had suddenly gotten a lot less attractive. She was clearly just a religious nutter like the rest of the Keres at times. He understood the appeal of believing in the Genetrix rubbish but he wanted everyone to focus on what was really happening instead of believing in Gods and Goddesses that wouldn't save them.

"He doesn't believe in the Mother," Piper said.

Ithane smiled. "I can sense that and Spero is telling me that you're a good man. But I don't understand why Genetrix and Geneitor have brought us together on this planet,"

"Does it matter?" Jerico asked. "I'm only here because a dying friend made me promise to find you, make sure you're okay and give you this,"

Jerico took off the necklace and he was surprised how sad he felt that he was giving up the necklace. But he was a soldier, a fighter and a survivor. He had done his mission and he was done, he didn't need to get involved in this battle.

Jerico went to past the necklace to Ithane when she shook her head and whipped out her swords.

"What?" Piper asked.

"Dark Keres incoming," Ithane said.

Jerico had no idea how this woman could possibly know that but moments later three black portals opened.

Nothing came out.

Jerico aimed his machine gun at the portals but then they closed.

"What was that?" Jerico asked.

"They were watching us," Piper said.

"No," Ithane said shaking her head and Jerico had to admit she was hot as hell when she looked all serious and wise. "Geneitor wanted to see the three of us. I felt his cold stare look at us but I don't understand any of this,"

Jerico looked around and thankfully the smoky black sky was clear of enemies for now. He just didn't know how long that would last.

"What the hell is going on here?" Jerico asked.

Ithane smiled. "I think Genetrix and Geneitor have somehow twisted the fates of millions to bring us all here,"

"Why?" Jerico asked hating this damn divine game and rubbish. "Why bring together Dark Keres, whatever you are and Imperials together? What could a Great Mother and the thousands of Keres on this planet bring this so-called Death God?"

Jerico noticed Ithane was staring right at him like he had said something extremely serious.

"Oh Genetrix," Piper said. "I was so stupid. Why didn't I see it earlier,"

"We're seeing it now," Ithane said.

"What?" Jerico asked hearing the roaring of Imperial engines in the distance.

"When the Treaty of Defeat was signed," Ithane said, "the Keres split into four fractions shortly afterwards. The Dark Keres were Keres and humans that fell to the worship of Geneitor and they want to bring around the resurrection,"

"So he can apparently bring around the end of all life," Jerico said.

"Then there are the Daughters of Genetrix," Ithane said. "That want to protect all life. But there are the *normal* Keres that live in Keres society under the extreme oppression of Imperial rule in all but name,"

"So?" Jerico asked knowing the enemy were getting a lot closer.

"So," Piper said, "there is a final fraction. A fraction no one talks about and everyone thought they were dead. I've lived with them so hundreds of years so I had forgotten how mysterious we were to the rest of you,"

"The Protectors," Ithane said," were some of the most important Keres in the entire galaxy. They all left for the Mother World of Genesis and they are so powerful their souls burn brightest in the entire species and they were guarding two Soulstones,"

Jerico nodded. He didn't believe in the Soulstone crap but clearly the Imperium and the Dark Keres did. And he was willing to bet these so-called Soulstones were in the tunnels, exactly where thousands of innocent Keres were hiding.

Thousands of innocents that were about to get killed.

"I saw the Soulstones once," Piper said.

Ithane glared at her and Jerico had no idea why that was so important.

"Describe them quickly. I might be able to identify them," Ithane said.

"Um they were both black. One had a red swirl in and another one had a sickly green swirl that was laughing at me constantly," Piper said.

"Shit. Shit. Shit," Ithane said. "Those Soulstones belong to Geneitor. He birthed the Gods of Plague and the God of Rage. If his followers get their hands on them then they are two steps closer to resurrecting him,"

Jerico wasn't sure if that was true but as he saw three enemy bombers heading straight for them he didn't care.

"We have to get to the tunnels now!" Jerico shouted.

Ithane nodded and she waved her sexy arms in the air and another portal opened. Jerico wasn't sure about going inside but the roar of a bomb dropping towards them made him decide.

He leapt through the portal and just hoped beyond hope he wasn't going to die.

CHAPTER 11

I was surprised as hell when I appeared on top of a massive purple crystal tower in the middle of some impressive Keres city. I had always loved Keres cities because like this one, they were so artful, massive and stunning.

But I could sense the fear, desperation and death that was sweeping over the city. I noticed there was some kind of cloaking magic in effect so with a thought I switched it off and just grinned as I saw the Great Mother.

I immediately bowed as I saw the kind cheerful-looking Keres woman in her robes and staff. She waved me to stop me and instead she bowed.

Then I noticed the five dead guards around her and the blood dripping from her staff.

"What happened?" beautiful Jerico said and I couldn't blame him. This was serious.

"Geneitor got to them," the Great Mother said. "He tried to corrupt me too but I resisted him. He promised me wonders, entire planets and entire slave armies to myself but I declined,"

I nodded and I couldn't believe any of this. I knew Geneitor was more conscious than Genetrix and his followers had more power but I had never seen him *this* focused on a planet before.

And as much as I didn't want to, I didn't believe it was all because of the Soulstones. There was something larger going on here and I needed to know what.

"How long has this battle been going on for?" I asked.

"No idea," Jerico said. "All the clocks have stopped. Communications don't work and even the Keres' magic has been spotty. Speaking of which I didn't think humans could use magic,"

I smiled. "Genetrix resurrected me so I'm a mixture of Keres and human. That isn't important now,"

I paced around and that was serious. I presumed the Keres were using their clocks that were connected to reality itself. No one could stop them unless they were being disconnected from reality.

I didn't know that was possible. Maybe it wasn't but something was making this world warped and twisted and strange like I had never seen it before.

Then it hit me.

"The souls. The fucking souls!" I shouted understanding everything that was going on here.

"What?" Jerico asked checking the skies for any

enemy aircraft.

I paced around a little. "Geneitor made the Dark Keres, the Imperial and the Protectors all come to this planet at this moment together so he could create a war like no other,"

A deafening explosion echoed all around me and I saw the screams of a thousand souls echo all around me.

"And think about the types of Souls Geneitor made come here," Piper said. "Human souls are like tealights but he brought a Hand Of the Rex and her special forces,"

I nodded. That made perfect sense. Even if millions of humans died here, their souls would only be worth the power of a hundred or a thousand Keres souls. But if Geneitor brought more powerful souls here like a Hand of the Rex then that would be a feast for him.

"Okay," Jerico said. "So he wants to create a massive war. To what end?"

I shut off the sound of the screaming souls that filled my senses and I just laughed at that handsome man. He was so cute in his naivety about the divine chess game he was entering.

"Why else would a Death God want as many souls as he could get?" I asked. "He wants to feast and he wants to unleash his two children on this planet."

Everyone went silent and I felt the purple tower shake underneath us.

Piper swallowed hard. "Are you telling me that if enough souls are devoured here than Geneitor can resurrect two of his Demi-Gods?"

"Yes," I said. "And they will walk the stars once more as they did back in the Old War,"

I shivered. I couldn't believe this was happening but it was true. It was all damn true and I had been so stupid as to fall for it.

"I've brought the entirety of the Daughters Of Genetrix. Two million Keres and humans on my fleet just sitting there waiting to die,"

My hands formed fists. I was meant to protect them. I was meant to save them. And I hated to imagine how many thousands of them had died already for my mistake.

Jerico gently rubbed my shoulder and I loved his warm skin against my armour.

"We can fix this," Jerico said holding up his necklace. "Can this Spero thing help us?"

I grinned as I stared into the bright golden light of Spero God of Hope. I felt a great sense of wonderfully warm hope fill my soul and images filled my mind. Spero was showing me images of life, death and the tunnels. He showed me an image of a massive golden portal and the Keres leaving through it.

He had to be telling me about portalling the Keres off the planet and onto my ships. I didn't even know if my ships could escape but I had to try.

Every life spared was a life Geneitor couldn't use to fuel his foul demi-gods.

I looked at the Great Mother and the horrible aroma of blood, death and decay filled my nose. Something was happening so I was going to have to be quick.

"You said your magic was affected. How?" I asked the Great Mother and Piper.

"I don't know," Piper said, "but I feel cutoff from Genetrix. I feel like her magical presence is through a dense fog and every time I try to reach out to her I get lost in the fog,"

"That would work," I said grinning because I knew exactly how I was going to save everyone but I needed Jerico's help.

I smiled at Jerico and for some reason he smiled back. His grin was beautiful and I was so looking forward to getting to know him better if he survived this.

"What you thinking?" Jerico asked.

"I'm going to break the fog for everyone and save their lives," I said.

Pure happiness filled me and I just hoped I could save everyone.

Little did I realise just how impossible that was going to be.

CONVERGENCE OF ODYSSEYS

CHAPTER 12

"You need to buy me as much time as possible," Ithane said.

Jerico just nodded as he checked his machine gun and liked the sheer weight of it in his hands. He was going to light up the immense cavern they were in and he was going to make the enemy pay whenever they showed up.

"My Lady," the Great Mother said to Ithane, "everyone is here,"

Jerico looked behind him and just gasped as he realised just how immense the cavern truly was. There were thousands upon thousands of male and female Keres here in thin robes. They were all lined up in neat rows and Jerico felt sorry for them as he saw fear, pain and terror on their faces.

They believed they were going to die here.

Jerico was surprised the cavern was large enough to fit everyone inside but it was. The smell of death, decay and rotting flesh filled the air and Jerico supposed that could have been caused by the so-called Plague God hiding down here.

"Jerico," Ithane said and Jerico's heart skipped a few beats, "when I start the ritual and the Keres start portalling away the enemy will come. Geneitor will know exactly where we are and he will send his followers to kill me,"

Jerico nodded at Ithane and weakly smiled at Piper and a group of ten Keres warriors came over to him.

"Your job is to keep the enemy back as long as you can," Ithane said.

"Of course," Jerico said. "I've fought in enough wars to know how to defend people,"

"I fear sooner or later won't be fighting Keres or humans," Ithane said.

The entire cavern jerked violently and immense chunks of rock collapsed from the ceiling. Smashing down and killing some Keres below.

"They're here," the Great Mother said taking out her staff.

Jerico watched as Ithane rushed over to a large opening at the edge of the cavern next to the massive staircase they had all entered from.

He was tempted to move over there and protect the staircase but he didn't believe for a second the enemy were going to use stairs to enter the cavern. He hated magic.

Ithane raised her arms and hands and her long beautiful hair flowed all around her like some angel.

The entire cavern shook violently again. Jerico's fingers tightened around the trigger. He looked at Piper and her warriors and they nodded back at him.

They were ready for whatever was coming.

"Brothers and sisters," Ithane said as the air crackled with white magical energy, "reach out into the void and seek the magical touch of the Goddess of Life, our most holy mother,"

Jerico noticed no one looked convinced and he really didn't like the icy cold sensation coming from Spero. Maybe it was a warning.

"The Mother is not lost beyond the fog," Ithane said. "She is there and she is ready to give us her strength. I am here with you, her Will Incarnate, on Genesis. The brightness of my soul will create a bridge to her divine touch,"

Jerico wasn't convinced but he saw most of the Keres were smiling and they were closing their eyes and concentrating.

"We cannot allow the Keres to lose that focus," Jerico said to Piper as the air started crackling with black energy.

"Reach out brothers and sisters! See the Mother in the void. Let her touch your soul and give you the magic you were destined to have!" Ithane shouted.

A loud bang filled the cavern and humming and vibrating echoed all around Jerico. Golden portals opened in front of some of the Keres then more and more. They stepped through.

And Jerico realised it was going to take a while to

evacuate the thousands of Keres to the Daughter of Genetrix ships.

Time they didn't have.

"They're coming!" Ithane shouted.

Jerico spun around as black portals opened on the ceiling.

He aimed his machine gun. He fired.

Bullets screamed through the air.

Corrupted humans with charred skin rained down on the cavern.

Jerico fired.

Exploding heads.

Exploding chests.

Demonic blood rained down upon them.

Jerico hissed as the blood burnt his skin.

Jerico kept firing.

He had to protect everyone here. He had to fire to the last.

He had to make sure as many Keres survived this attack.

He had a feeling the fate of the galaxy depended on it.

CHAPTER 13

The thick foul aromas of death, rotting flesh and disease filled my senses as Geneitor tried to corrupt me and make me lose focus. How dare the bastard threaten to stop me from my holy mission. I hope all his servants got slaughtered by Jerico, Piper and their noble warriors.

I had to close my eyes from the battle in the cavern as I focused on what was happening in the magical realm. The magical reflection of reality that all magic played in.

I could see Genesis burn, crack and smoke veil its once beautiful blue sky. I wanted to shout, scream and vow revenge on Geneitor for despoiling the most precious planet in the galaxy, but I had to focus.

To my left I could see a thick cloud of magical fog with thousands upon thousands of screaming, laughing and singing faces with teeth just slashing at me. Geneitor had cut off the Keres from Genetrix's touch and those demons in the fog wanted souls to eat.

I had already purged enough of the demons to create a small tunnel for the Keres to reach out through and Genetrix could gift them her magic again. But I could feel the pressure of Geneitor's corruption pressing against my mind.

A headache corkscrewed across my forehead and I wasn't sure how long I could keep this up for. Geneitor was pissed as hell and he wanted me dead.

My skin grew colder and small shards of ice started to cover my skin. Genetrix couldn't protect me much longer from Geneitor's focus and I knew he would find my exact location in this magical realm very soon.

"Go Mother," I said, "save your children and let me deal with the Father of Death,"

I felt Genetrix pulse cold and then warmth into me like she was struggling to decide but a moment later I felt the warmth leave me. I was alone for a little bit and I just had to make sure I was still alive when Genetrix refocused on me.

If I died now she wouldn't be able to find my soul and resurrect me again.

"Show yourself Geneitor," I said and smiled as the demons in the fogs stopped slashing their teeth.

Hopefully that would give the Keres more time to escape and I would be able to focus on the Death God instead of protecting the Keres'.

"You look different my Child," a deep booming voice said.

I looked around for the voice but I couldn't see anything. My headache got a thousand times worse and it took everything I had not to collapse to my knees.

"Do you like my handy work Child?" Geneitor asked. "Do you like how I twisted the fate of millions to bring them all here so I can get revenge?"

"Don't you mean resurrect your children?"

The entire magical realm went silent for a moment and I was shocked. My headache got a lot better and I couldn't understand this.

"You didn't know?" I asked. "How can the Death God not know when his demi-gods are on the world he is burning?"

Then I realised that was the least of my problems. I had been working on the assumption that Geneitor was only doing all of this to bring back two of his children so they could burn the galaxy and kill in his name once more as they walked the stars.

If he didn't do all of this for those reasons then why the hell was he burning a planet to ash?

"That is most interesting Child. Are you sure you work for the Mother of Life? You have been most helpful to me as well so I thank you,"

"You are nothing," I said as I managed to feel his presence behind me.

I whipped out my two swords. I spun around.

I smashed into the swords of a giant with four arms with a double-ended sword in each hand. The air around him crackled with black energy and I knew

I was looking at one of the major forms of Geneitor.

He wasn't hiding from me this time. This was what he actually looked like.

He wore an immensely long robe that looked a thousand years old judging by the holes and how shredded it was. His face was covered by a black hood but I could feel his piercing glaze look into my soul.

"Such a tasty looking soul you have there. How many Demi-gods do you think you are worth? A hundred? A thousand? A million? Let me taste you and find out!"

He swung at me.

I tried to block. I couldn't.

He smashed his swords into me.

Throwing me back tens of metres.

He ran after me.

Slamming his legs into me.

He kicked me to the ground.

I smashed onto a ground that wasn't there.

Black magical rope wrapped itself around my neck.

It tightened. I gasped. He laughed.

I shot out my hand.

No magic came out.

Geneitor went to kiss me.

I screamed out in terror.

I swung my sword.

Slicing his cheek.

He hissed.

He released me.

I thrusted out my hands.

White fire shot out of them.

Geneitor absorbed it all and charged at me.

I tried to block.

I couldn't.

He kicked me.

Pinning me against a ground that wasn't there.

"Do you think you are the first incarnate of Genetrix's Will? Do you think you are so special that you will even be the last,"

I laughed. "I don't care if I was the thousandth or millionth Incarnate. I serve Genetrix and your time is done,"

"How Child? I am burning this planet, freeing my children and I will devour your soul before I am done with you,"

"No you won't," I said grinning, "because you forget unlike you I am not bound to this realm so I just have to open my eyes and I am free of this place,"

Geneitor roared. He swung his swords.

I opened my eyes.

CHAPTER 14

Jerico flat out hated these damn abominations as he fired his machine gun endlessly inside the immense cavern. Corrupted humans with black veiny rotting flesh kept coming down from the ceiling.

He fired again and again.

Jerico hated how the smell of death, rotting flesh and blood filled his senses and the taste of iron formed on his tongue. He kept firing.

He wasn't allowing the enemy to win here.

Jerico smiled as he kept purging the enemy as Piper and her warriors howled like wolves. They charged around the caverns running like the steep walls of the cavern was flat ground.

They swirled, twirled and slaughtered the enemy as they poured out of the portals.

Click went the trigger. Click. Click. Click.

Jerico hissed as he threw his machine gun at the head of a corrupted human as it landed in front of him.

The black portals crackled and Jerico's eyes widened as tens upon tens of Dark Keres stormed out of them. The humans had only attacked to get rid of his weapons and his ammo.

Jerico looked around.

He rushed over to a Keres sword on the floor. He grabbed it.

The Great Mother rushed over. White fire shooting out of her hands.

Jerico spun around. There were tens of Dark Keres landing on the ground now. They fired at the escaping Keres.

Jerico flew forward.

Swinging his sword.

Hacking the enemy apart.

Blood sprayed up walls. Brain matter exploded out. Flesh burnt.

There were too many.

A Dark Keres landed on top of Jerico. Knocking his sword away.

Jerico fell to the ground. He punched the Dark Keres. He kicked. He struggled.

It was useless.

The Dark Keres pinned his arms with evil magic. Jerico tried to move. He couldn't.

His necklace glowed bright white.

The Dark Keres screamed in terror.

Jerico grabbed the Keres's neck and snapped it.

He leapt up and used the Dark Keres's gun to slaughter three more enemies descending on the escaping Keres.

They were simply too many foes.

Three corpses of Piper's warriors landed around him.

This battle was lost. It was always lost. And Jerico just wanted to protect Ithane.

He rushed over to her. Her eyes were closed and the air was still crackling white light around her. Whatever she was doing he really hoped she was going to hurry the hell up.

A roar came from behind him.

Jerico swung around.

Beheading a Dark Keres.

Then the Dark Keres just stopped and Jerico prepared to strike as three of the enemy dropped down in front of him.

Jerico didn't understand why the enemy were stopping and they were simply allowing the Keres to escape through their golden portals.

The cavern shook violently.

Then it stopped.

Jerico hated the strange silence that washed over the cavern like a wave. He tried to stomp his feet on the ground but no sound came from it.

Then Jerico just looked at the Dark Keres in front of him and they just grinned as they snapped their own necks and laughed as they died.

"What the hell is going on?" Jerico asked surprised his words formed sounds.

The Great Mother was about to speak when the

ground collapsed from under her and she screamed in agony as she was murdered.

Jerico moved away and really hoped Ithane would snap out of it soon. He needed her. He needed that beautiful woman back.

"Commander! The hole," Piper shouted still on the walls of the cavern.

Jerico pointed his sword at the hole where the Great Mother had been as four long hands with claw-like fingers appeared and then a humanoid person pulled themselves up.

Jerico's eyes widened as he looked at the extremely tall Keres male (maybe four metres tall) in thick green rotting, rusty armour with flies, maggots and puss oozing from him.

The man grinned at Jerico and Jerico wanted to scream at the man's black teeth, rotting tongue and sheer corruption. This wasn't natural at all and Jerico hated it.

"It is good to walk once more," the man said with flies pouring out of his mouth as he spoke.

Jerico wanted to be sick.

"Yes little human. Be sick, vomit, let me bathe in your sickness," the man said.

"Oh shit," Jerico said as he realised this was the God of Plague. It couldn't be and Jerico didn't want to believe it but he couldn't deny what he was seeing.

He was actually seeing a Keres God in front of him.

The God Of Plague grinned as he looked at all

the escaping Keres and he clicked his fingers.

All the golden portals turned sickly green and the Keres screamed in agony as they entered by mistake. Jerico had no doubt they were becoming twisted, diseased and corrupted beyond recognition.

The God Of Plague shivered like he had just had the best sex in the universe.

Jerico pointed his sword at the God's throat. "Stop this,"

"I will not little human. I am a God and I am the creator of disease and I am giving these Keres a chance to live and serve the True God once more,"

Jerico charged at the God.

Piper tackled Jerico to the ground.

The Plague God thrusted out his hands.

Millions of flies zoomed towards the remaining Keres besides Piper and devoured their flesh. Then the flies disappeared.

Thousands of Keres dead in a single moment.

"Don't worry human and Keres," the Plague God said. "I will turn you into my Greatest Disease Spreaders ever!"

"No you will not!" Ithane shouted.

And Jerico just grinned because he couldn't help but believe shit was about to go down.

That both excited and terrified him way more than he ever wanted to admit.

CHAPTER 15

This was bad. This was so bloody bad. This was the worst thing ever.

I just glared at the twisted, diseased, rotting corpse of the Plague God as I pointed my swords at his chest. I couldn't fight a God. This wasn't my domain and my wheelhouse. All I wanted to do was survive and help Jerico and Piper escape from this damn planet and this cavern.

The cavern was charred and wrecked and I noticed there were thousands of flies and maggots starting to pour down from the ceiling.

The Plague God was actually starting to corrupt the very planet itself. I didn't want Piper or Jerico here any longer than they had to be because sooner or later he would start to corrupt their souls. Something I couldn't allow.

I flew at the Plague God.

I swung my swords.

I slashed at him.

I lashed.

He laughed.

He dodged.

He kicked me.

I charged at him.

He screamed.

Unleashing swarms upon swarms of flies at me.

Fire shot out of my hands.

The Plague God charged at Jerico.

Jerico slashed his sword.

Slicing into the Plague God's face.

Slugs and snails poured out of the wound and then it healed itself.

The Plague God clapped his hands and slugs covered our skin.

I burnt them away and then Jerico and Piper collapsed to the ground and started vomiting.

"Stop this!" I shouted.

"Never," the Plague God said. "I want them to throw up their organs. I want them to give me something warm to wipe on my skin,"

"You're disgusting,"

"I am the Plague God. I am the beginning and the end of all life. I am the killer that lurks in the air you breathe, the water you drink and the food you eat,"

I charged him.

The Plague God clicked his fingers.

I was smashed against a maggot-covered wall.

I burnt the maggots away and I felt a headache

form in my mind. The temperature dropped so much that my breath formed vapour.

Something was coming.

We had to escape now but I couldn't open a portal with the Plague God here in case he corrupted it or followed us to my ship.

I just grinned because there was only one hope for our survival. I had to summon Vita, the avatar of Genetrix.

"You look hopeful for a change," the Plague God said. "What happened?"

The entire planet shook and jerked and cracked.

Immense chunks of rock collapsed from the ceiling. Something was happening to the planet.

"I'm hijacking the souls of the dead. Come to me Vita, avatar of the Goddess of Life," I said.

The Plague God laughed. "Genetrix has no avatar,"

"You have been banished way too long to realise what Her power truly is,"

The Plague God clicked his fingers and all the millions of flies and maggots on the walls laughed as they formed into humanoid creatures with puss and disease oozing from their pores.

"Kill her," the Plague God said.

I just grinned as a bright white portal appeared. The Plague God tried to corrupt it but he couldn't. This was a portal made by the souls of the dead and the damned.

A massive Keres female stepped out of the portal

with bright white light shining from her. Choirs of angels echoed around the cavern and I just grinned as her long golden hair burnt bright with righteousness.

Vita looked at the Plague God and she screamed in rage.

She flew at the God.

Swords swung.

Swords clashed.

Earthquakes boomed from the fighting.

I rushed over to Jerico and Piper who were vomiting and gasping for air.

I shone white healing light from my hands and purified them and their mind and their souls.

"We have to get out of here," Jerico said.

The planet cracked and jerked and shook. The cavern's floor started to collapse.

I grabbed Jerico's and Piper's arm and I teleported us out of there.

I just hoped beyond hope we could escape the orbit in time.

CHAPTER 16

Jerico flat out hated the foul taste of bile, rot and disease that filled his mouth as he materialised on a large oval bridge of some spaceship he didn't recognise. He liked how beautiful Ithane threw him and Piper onto the same large metal command throne but that was where everything went to hell.

The entire bridge was a hive of activity. Ithane was pointing and shouting and barking orders like their lives depended on it.

It probably did.

Jerico watched as Genesis was glowing bright black and the ground looked like it was ripping itself apart. Even the Imperial and Dark Keres warships around the planet looked like they were trying to flee but they were exploding.

Whatever ship Jerico was on shook, vibrated and popped.

Jerico fell to one side as he tried to get up but Piper grabbed him and forced him to sit down on the command throne. He wanted to start reading the data outputs that were probably in the command throne but he didn't know how to work this tech.

"Fucking hell!" a human woman shouted.

Jerico looked at Genesis as an immense black portal with bright white edges opened to the left of the planet and Genesis just shattered.

The entire planet cracked like an egg and the entire world turned to ash.

The portal sucked the planet inside and then Jerico was forced off the command throne as the ship jerked.

"It's pulling us inside," someone said.

"Get us into Ultraspace now!" Ithane shouted.

"Negative," a human woman said with a nametag saying April.

"Look," Piper said.

Jerico looked out into the coldness of the void and his eyes just widened as the Imperial ships opened Ultraspace portals and as they went into Ultraspace. They exploded.

Ithane gripped her head and Jerico had no idea what this was like for her. He didn't know if she was hearing the screaming souls of the dying but this had to be overwhelming for her.

The ship banged and spun as something smashed into it.

Jerico gripped the command throne as the entire bridge spun around them.

"Get us into the Nexus now!" Ithane shouted.

The ship's engines hummed violently. They sounded like they were about to explode.

Jerico couldn't see anything but splashes of explosions, fires and death outside.

Something exploded on the ship. Screams filled the bridge. Warning alarms filled Jerico's head. He didn't know what was happening.

The ship jerked a final time and Jerico's world went black as something smashed into the side of his head.

CHAPTER 17

The loud deafening beeping of warning alarms, the sound of crying and people in pain filled Jerico's ears as he woke up moments later. His vision was a blur of bright white light with some black lines as he assumed some people were moving around him.

The smell of vapourised blood and burning rubber and ozone filled his senses and Jerico wanted to be sick. But he didn't dare allow himself, he didn't want the awful taste of bile in his mouth ever again.

After a few moments Jerico's vision cleared and he partly wished it hadn't when he saw what had happened. The bridge was covered in the twisted bodies of humans and Keres with their dark rich red blood painting the floor, command consoles and computers.

He saw Ithane sitting on the floor, tears pouring down her beautiful cheeks and he just wanted to hug her. Ithane was holding her head and trying to cover her ears with her arms but Jerico could tell it wasn't working.

Jerico forced himself up and he was relieved to see Piper was alive and talking to a human man behind them. Piper had blood all over her and he really hoped she was going to be okay.

"Ithane," Jerico said going over to her and sitting in front of her. "Are you okay?"

"It won't stop. The screams won't stop. I can hear them. Every single person that died on Genesis and around it. I can hear them all,"

Jerico felt a wave of emotion wash over him. He couldn't even begin to know what it was like and he was fairly sure he didn't want to know. So he took off the necklace and placed it on Ithane's lap and was relieved when she smiled a little. Spero glowed a little brighter so hopefully he was taking some of the burden away from her.

Jerico hated seeing such a beautiful, strong and amazing warrior in pain.

"How many did we lose?" Jerico asked.

Ithane stopped crying immediately and frowned. "Everyone. This is the only ship that survived the attack. We have a crew of five thousand and we managed to take two thousand refugees from the planet,"

"Out of twenty thousand," April said who was sitting down next to them.

Jerico nodded his hellos to her but April didn't look interested.

"My Lady," April said, "there was a problem

when you were away. There was a plague that was unleashed on the entire fleet. We fought it and won but the mortality rate was extreme,"

Jerico could see Ithane couldn't take much more bad news but she was trying to be strong for her forces. Jerico could see how much everyone loved her, worshipped her and wanted to please her. But he could see none of this was easy for her.

He didn't want to be here and he didn't want to be in her shoes, but he was involved now. He had seen some Plague God brought back from the dead and he wanted revenge. He didn't wish that vomiting trick on anyone.

"What happened out there?" Jerico asked.

"Please excuse me my Lady," April said. "I need to double-check my calculations. The Nexus isn't as safe as it once was to traverse,"

"Thank you April I mean it," Ithane said giving her friend a weak smile before turning back to Jerico. "This was a mistake,"

"What happened out there? How the hell does an entire planet just shatter like glass?" Jerico asked.

Jerico noticed Ithane didn't say anything until a group of engineers had finished walking past.

Ithane leant in closer. "Geneitor isn't an idiot. He didn't know about the two Soulstones on Genesis. He got the Imperium there, he got us there and he got his servants there just to weaken us all,"

Jerico nodded. That made perfect sense and he loved military strategy as much as the next commander but this was extreme. Geneitor had clearly wanted to destroy the Imperium and the Daughters of Genetrix, but why do it this way?

So Jerico asked Ithane.

"Because when mainstream Keres society learn of this. They will be angry as hell and they will put a lot of pressure on their Sovereign to rip up the Treaty of Defeat,"

"Geneitor wants another Human-Keres war," Jerico said. "So more people will die and he gets more souls to feast on. What happened to the Soulstones?"

Ithane laughed. "You really think the destruction of a planet by Geneitor stops the Soulstones. He has them both now and his Plague God can walk amongst the stars sowing death, disease and plague wherever he goes,"

Ithane stood up and Jerico followed her to the large circular door that led away from the bridge.

"I'm sorry you got caught up in all this," Ithane said smiling. "If you tell me where you want to be dropped off, I'll make it happen,"

"What?" Jerico asked not understanding why Ithane thought he wouldn't want to fight alongside her (and spend even more time with this beautiful woman).

"This isn't your fight and the chances of you surviving this are basically nothing," Ithane said grabbing his hand. "You gave me Spero and he will be a massive help,"

Jerico loved the smooth warmth of her small

hand in his. He loved the flow of electricity between them. He couldn't leave her just yet, if ever.

"Will me joining this fight save lives?" Jerico asked knowing the answer.

"Of course,"

"Then I am staying. I fought in the Imperial army to protect humanity and that is why I came to find you. I might not have believed in this God rubbish until an hour ago but I want to fight now,"

Ithane passed Jerico his Spero necklace again. "The God of Hope chose you to be his wearer, let us not dishonour the will of the Gods,"

Jerico gasped as Ithane kissed his cheek and his wayward parts exploded to life at the sheer chemistry that flowed between them. Jerico seriously wanted to get to know her better.

And he was joining this fight and ship of humans and Keres, he was finally going to get the chance to make a difference, be with the woman he seriously liked and hopefully help to make the galaxy a safer place.

A perfect end to a weird odyssey.

CHAPTER 18

When I went into my large office in the deepest sections of the *Lady of Light*, I couldn't help but frown at the sheer destruction of my once beautiful office. There used to be wonderful purple crystals that covered the dirty walls of the office in their millions, and each one represented a small soul of an agent or spy or servant of Genetrix out in the galaxy.

But they were all mostly shattered and the foul smell of death, burnt flesh and strawberries overwhelmed me. I hated what Geneitor had done to my office and I almost couldn't believe what had happened today.

I was glad my old wooden desk had survived so I sat on top of it, and I simply laid down. I allowed the warmth of the desk to pulse into my body and I almost smiled at the nice comfort the warmth provided, because today had been a mistake and a half.

The ceiling was still covered a good enough

amount of purple crystals that pulsed warmly and if I focused on a crystal I could weakly hear the mutterings and talking of my spies across the galaxy.

Everyone was starting to learn about the annihilation of Genesis, and I had little doubt I would get thousands of messages in the next few days begging me for new orders. My spies would want to help and maybe I would get new recruits for my network and fleet, but I had no idea if I could protect them.

I had come here with every single ship I had and now I only had one left. That was a stupid mistake.

I wasn't even sure what my next moves were because I was out of ideas. Genesis was dead, the Plague God had returned and Geneitor himself had another Soulstone and I only had one single stone. It wasn't like I could use Spero as much as I wanted to because I was still human at heart. I didn't live and breathe the ancient myths and texts about the Gods and Goddesses.

But I had to learn sooner or later or everyone would be killed by Geneitor.

Someone knocked on my door.

With a thought I opened the door to my office and I smiled when Piper and April came in. I had wanted Jerico to join us but the rest of the crew were enjoying learning from him and his tactical knowledge. He was a beautiful man and I was so happy he had decided to stay with us.

I was so, so looking forward to spending more

time with him.

Piper and April were both in the light blue robes of the Navigators and I was happy that Piper had found a role for herself so soon.

"How's our course through the Nexus?" I asked.

"We aren't being followed and the entire Nexus might be shifting in ways I've never seen before but I've plotted a safe course for us. I still need a destination," April said.

I laughed. "Where the hell can we go? We cannot go to the Imperium because we're traitors and extremists to them. We cannot go to the Keres because they believe in the Treaty of Defeat more than the truth of the situation. And our list of friends are short,"

Piper nodded. "Then we go to the Enlightened Republic and hope they can protect us for a while,"

I had to admit that wasn't a bad idea. The Enlightened Republic was a small group of breakaway systems that believed in freedom, democracy and goodness unlike the Imperium. They had been good to my network before so I nodded.

April went to turn away but I gently grabbed her arm.

"What happened today requires power I have never seen before," I said. "Geneitor is growing more powerful by the day and I think we have to accept that his resurrection is an extremely real possibility in the next few years,"

"I thought that wouldn't be a possibility for

centuries," April said.

"I would have agreed with you yesterday," I said coldly, "but today... today was a turning point in the web of fate. Geneitor twisted the odyssey of millions so he would get them to converge on Genesis at the same time,"

"But," Piper said stretching her arms, "my question is, why did he allow your odyssey and Jerico's odyssey to converge? Together you two are extremely dangerous to him, but allow you two to cross paths,"

After a minute of me not replying the two women bowed slightly and left my office, and I went back to lying on my wonderfully warm desk. I had a small theory about that but I wasn't going to tell them because it was dangerous as hell.

I strongly believe that Geneitor wanted me and Jerico to meet because I think he's arrogant enough to want a real challenger. Him and Genetrix could play their little game for a thousand years and not really damage or hurt each other, but I think Geneitor's growing bored in Ultraspace and I think he wants to play.

But he could easily wipe us out and resurrect himself if he allowed himself to deny his servants even the smallest fraction of free will. I think he wanted me and Jerico to meet so he could prolong the game a little longer and make it a little more fun.

A costly mistake for him because I fully intended to save my forces, rally my supporters and we were going to find all five Soulstones belonging to Genetrix so she can kick his ass once and for all.

And that wasn't a threat, it was a promise.

GET YOUR FREE SHORT STORY NOW!
And get signed up to Connor Whiteley's newsletter to hear about new gripping books, offers and exciting projects. (You'll never be sent spam)
https://www.subscribepage.io/garrosignup

About the author:

Connor Whiteley is the author of over 60 books in the sci-fi fantasy, nonfiction psychology and books for writer's genre and he is a Human Branding Speaker and Consultant.

He is a passionate warhammer 40,000 reader, psychology student and author.

Who narrates his own audiobooks and he hosts The Psychology World Podcast.

All whilst studying Psychology at the University of Kent, England.

Also, he was a former Explorer Scout where he gave a speech to the Maltese President in August 2018 and he attended Prince Charles' 70th Birthday Party at Buckingham Palace in May 2018.

Plus, he is a self-confessed coffee lover!

<u>Other books by Connor Whiteley:</u>
<u>Bettie English Private Eye Series</u>
A Very Private Woman
The Russian Case
A Very Urgent Matter
A Case Most Personal
Trains, Scots and Private Eyes
The Federation Protects
Cops, Robbers and Private Eyes
Just Ask Bettie English
An Inheritance To Die For
The Death of Graham Adams
Bearing Witness
The Twelve
The Wrong Body
The Assassination Of Bettie English
Wining And Dying
Eight Hours
Uniformed Cabal
A Case Most Christmas

<u>Gay Romance Novellas</u>
Breaking, Nursing, Repairing A Broken Heart
Jacob And Daniel
Fallen For A Lie
Spying And Weddings
Clean Break

Awakening Love
Meeting A Country Man
Loving Prime Minister
Snowed In Love
Never Been Kissed
Love Betrays You

Lord of War Origin Trilogy:
Not Scared Of The Dark
Madness
Burn Them All

Way Of The Odyssey
Odyssey of Rebirth
Convergence of Odysseys

Lady Tano Fantasy Adventure Stories
Betrayal
Murder
Annihilation

The Fireheart Fantasy Series
Heart of Fire
Heart of Lies
Heart of Prophecy
Heart of Bones
Heart of Fate

CONVERGENCE OF ODYSSEYS

<u>City of Assassins (Urban Fantasy)</u>
City of Death
City of Martyrs
City of Pleasure
City of Power

<u>Agents of The Emperor</u>
Return of The Ancient Ones
Vigilance
Angels of Fire
Kingmaker
The Eight
The Lost Generation
Hunt
Emperor's Council
Speaker of Treachery
Birth Of The Empire
Terraforma
Spaceguard

<u>The Rising Augusta Fantasy Adventure Series</u>
Rise To Power
Rising Walls
Rising Force
Rising Realm

Lord Of War Trilogy (Agents of The Emperor)
Not Scared Of The Dark
Madness
Burn It All Down

Miscellaneous:
RETURN
FREEDOM
SALVATION
Reflection of Mount Flame
The Masked One
The Great Deer
English Independence

OTHER SHORT STORIES BY CONNOR WHITELEY

Mystery Short Story Collections
Criminally Good Stories Volume 1: 20 Detective Mystery Short Stories
Criminally Good Stories Volume 2: 20 Private Investigator Short Stories
Criminally Good Stories Volume 3: 20 Crime Fiction Short Stories
Criminally Good Stories Volume 4: 20 Science Fiction and Fantasy Mystery Short Stories

CONVERGENCE OF ODYSSEYS

Criminally Good Stories Volume 5: 20 Romantic Suspense Short Stories

<u>Connor Whiteley Starter Collections:</u>
Agents of The Emperor Starter Collection
Bettie English Starter Collection
Matilda Plum Starter Collection
Gay Romance Starter Collection
Way Of The Odyssey Starter Collection
Kendra Detective Fiction Starter Collection

<u>Mystery Short Stories:</u>
Protecting The Woman She Hated
Finding A Royal Friend
Our Woman In Paris
Corrupt Driving
A Prime Assassination
Jubilee Thief
Jubilee, Terror, Celebrations
Negative Jubilation
Ghostly Jubilation
Killing For Womenkind
A Snowy Death
Miracle Of Death
A Spy In Rome
The 12:30 To St Pancreas
A Country In Trouble

A Smokey Way To Go
A Spicy Way To GO
A Marketing Way To Go
A Missing Way To Go
A Showering Way To Go
Poison In The Candy Cane
Kendra Detective Mystery Collection Volume 1
Kendra Detective Mystery Collection Volume 2
Mystery Short Story Collection Volume 1
Mystery Short Story Collection Volume 2
Criminal Performance
Candy Detectives
Key To Birth In The Past

Science Fiction Short Stories:
Their Brave New World
Gummy Bear Detective
The Candy Detective
What Candies Fear
The Blurred Image
Shattered Legions
The First Rememberer
Life of A Rememberer
System of Wonder
Lifesaver

CONVERGENCE OF ODYSSEYS

Remarkable Way She Died
The Interrogation of Annabella Stormic
Blade of The Emperor
Arbiter's Truth
Computation of Battle
Old One's Wrath
Puppets and Masters
Ship of Plague
Interrogation
Edge of Failure

<u>Fantasy Short Stories:</u>
City of Snow
City of Light
City of Vengeance
Dragons, Goats and Kingdom
Smog The Pathetic Dragon
Don't Go In The Shed
The Tomato Saver
The Remarkable Way She Died
Dragon Coins
Dragon Tea
Dragon Rider

All books in 'An Introductory Series':
Clinical Psychology and Transgender Clients
Clinical Psychology
Careers In Psychology
Psychology of Suicide
Dementia Psychology
Clinical Psychology Reflections Volume 4
Forensic Psychology of Terrorism And Hostage-Taking
Forensic Psychology of False Allegations
Year In Psychology
CBT For Anxiety
CBT For Depression
Applied Psychology
BIOLOGICAL PSYCHOLOGY 3RD EDITION
COGNITIVE PSYCHOLOGY THIRD EDITION
SOCIAL PSYCHOLOGY- 3RD EDITION
ABNORMAL PSYCHOLOGY 3RD EDITION
PSYCHOLOGY OF RELATIONSHIPS- 3RD EDITION
DEVELOPMENTAL PSYCHOLOGY 3RD EDITION
HEALTH PSYCHOLOGY
RESEARCH IN PSYCHOLOGY

CONVERGENCE OF ODYSSEYS

A GUIDE TO MENTAL HEALTH AND TREATMENT AROUND THE WORLD- A GLOBAL LOOK AT DEPRESSION
FORENSIC PSYCHOLOGY
THE FORENSIC PSYCHOLOGY OF THEFT, BURGLARY AND OTHER CRIMES AGAINST PROPERTY
CRIMINAL PROFILING: A FORENSIC PSYCHOLOGY GUIDE TO FBI PROFILING AND GEOGRAPHICAL AND STATISTICAL PROFILING.
CLINICAL PSYCHOLOGY FORMULATION IN PSYCHOTHERAPY
PERSONALITY PSYCHOLOGY AND INDIVIDUAL DIFFERENCES
CLINICAL PSYCHOLOGY REFLECTIONS VOLUME 1
CLINICAL PSYCHOLOGY REFLECTIONS VOLUME 2
Clinical Psychology Reflections Volume 3
CULT PSYCHOLOGY
Police Psychology

www.ingramcontent.com/pod-product-compliance
Lightning Source LLC
LaVergne TN
LVHW012120070526
838202LV00056B/5803